"Gina, is that you? Gosh, I'm glad you called. It's been murder not talking to you all week. How's Hawaii? Meet any cool guys yet?"

I could tell her about Adam, I thought. No. But, there were Ron and Jim . . .

I launched into a tale about the great afternoon I'd spent with two fabulously cute rickshaw cabbies. I told Merry how they'd given me the grand tour and then invited me to a volleyball barbeque at the beach.

How could I sink so low? I'd lied to my very best friend, because I couldn't stand it that she had found a boyfriend and I hadn't.

Hawaiian Summer

by Cindy Savage

To Greg.

Cover photo by Gene Woolridge

Published by Willowisp Press, Inc.
401 E. Wilson Bridge Road, Worthington, Ohio 43085

Printed in the United States of America

10 9 8 7 6 5 4 3 2 1

ISBN 0-87406-304-3

One

"LOOK, Gina, there goes a shooting star. Let's make the promise again," Merry suggested. "Maybe wishing on a star will make it come true."

I twirled the pink string bracelet on my wrist. Merry had a matching bracelet tied around her wrist, too.

"It can't hurt," I replied.

Together we chanted. "I, Gina Louise Morgan . . ."

"I, Merry Taylor Jackson . . ."

". . . on this seventh day of July, swear to let only the first special boy who kisses me take off my bracelet."

We giggled, but quickly grew quiet. I stared out at the multicolored rowboats dotting Merrit Lake. Tomorrow I'd be looking at a different view—the crashing waves off Waikiki Beach in Honolulu, Hawaii.

This was my last night sitting on the shores of my favorite lake, wishing on shooting stars, and telling secrets to my best friend . . . for the rest of the summer.

"I'm not sure I'm going to like palm trees instead of weeping willows," I complained.

"Gina, you're going to love Hawaii," Merry said knowledgeably. She had been there for a week when she was ten. "There's so much to do. You'll learn the hula. You'll meet lots of cute guys on the beach. I'll bet you'll get your bracelet off first."

"No, you will, I'll bet."

"You're on," she said, giving me a high five. "I just wish I were going with *you* instead of having to wait until the middle of August to go with my family."

I sighed. A light breeze ruffled the grass. I lifted the heavy mass of strawberry blond curls off my neck and waited for the breeze to cool me off. I was excited about going to Hawaii, but I knew I wouldn't find a friend there like Merry Jackson. We're so much alike we could be identical twins, except that she's black and I'm white.

Everything else is the same, though. We have the same number of syllables in our names, and our birthdays are only three days apart. Mine's June fourth, and Merry's is June first. So we're both Geminis. And we both have shoulder-length, frizzy, curly hair. Mine's reddish blond, and hers is black.

We've known each other since we were babies. Our parents own a florist shop together. Sometimes we help create the arrangements that they send all over.

We're the same height, five feet six, too tall for any of the boys in the seventh grade. Hopefully, they'll grow by eighth. Hopefully, lots of things will happen before eighth grade begins in the fall.

I looked up at the stars again, remembering our promise. "I'm going to miss you, Merry," I told her.

She nodded in agreement as tears welled up in her brown and my green eyes. "Thank goodness for the telephone. I don't know what I'd do if I couldn't talk to you once a week."

"We'll tell each other everything."

"It'll be almost like there isn't even an ocean between us."

I jumped up, brushing the grass off my pants. "I'd better get going. My folks said we have to be in bed by nine o'clock," I explained reluctantly. "We leave from San Francisco International Airport at four o'clock in the morning. The flight's called the tired-eye or something."

"That's the red-eye," Merry said, laughing. "It's called that because people who travel all night instead of sleeping usually end up with red eyes."

We strolled slowly up the cobbled path from the lake to the apartment complex where we both lived. Neither of us wanted to say goodbye.

"I wish I were going with you," Merry said again, her lip pushed out in a pout. "You'll probably find a boyfriend before you even reach Hawaii. You'll have so many new faces to choose from, and I'll be stuck here with the same old *short* crowd from Oak Hills Junior High."

Two

MERRY was wrong. I didn't meet any prospective boyfriends on the airplane. Everybody was old or asleep. The flight attendant didn't even bother to wake most of the passengers up for the meal. It was chicken that tasted like cardboard, and it was pathetic.

While Mom and Dad and my brother, Stephen, slept, I stared out at the dark clouds. I tried to sleep, too. But I was too excited about actually seeing Hawaii.

When we finally arrived, it was only six o'clock local time, even though we had been flying for five hours.

What would living in Honolulu be like? I wondered for about the hundredth time as the wheels of the plane touched down on the runway. Merry had said there would be a lot to do. I hoped she was right. We were going to be living in my uncle Mark's condominium while he and his family were touring Europe. Dad had agreed to run Uncle Mark's business while they were away. It was a bicycle rickshaw and messenger service, and I was looking forward to a ride in one of the pedal-powered taxis.

I looked over at Stevie, who had managed to sleep peacefully the entire trip. I'd probably be stuck baby-sitting him for three months and never meet any guys at all. Who wants to talk to a girl on the beach who has her bratty little brother tagging along after her?

We gathered up our carry-on items and headed for the baggage claim area. I caught a glimpse of myself in the mirror next to the baggage carrousel. What a wreck! My hair was a mess. The tiny bit of mascara I'd put on before leaving California was smeared from leaning on my hand in the plane. My clothes looked like they hadn't been ironed in six months. And if that wasn't enough, I was falling asleep on my feet. I could sure see why they called that flight the *red-eye*.

"Welcome to Oahu!" the taxi driver boomed. He stowed our suitcases in the trunk of his beat-up green car. "Where to?"

I slumped in the backseat thinking about the shower I was going to take.

Dad looked at his watch. "Hey, it's going on seven o'clock. Let's swing by the shop on the way to Uncle Mark's. I'd like to get a look at the operation right away."

"Oh, Dad," I groaned. "Couldn't we go to Uncle Mark's first? I'm not in any shape to face the world."

"Nonsense," he said, not even looking at me. "You look fine. This won't take long, anyway. Then we can go home and get settled in."

Who could argue with Mr. Cheerful? I sank farther into the seat and tried to ignore Stevie's constant chatter about the beach, the sunrise, the mountains, the coconut trees, the hotels . . .

"Well, here we are!" announced the cabbie. "Want me to wait?"

"No, thanks. But if you'd like to swing by in a couple of hours, that would be great."

"Two hours! Dad!"

"Come on, Gina." Stevie yanked my arm in the direction of the wooden sign that read Ricki-Ticki Rickshaws—We'll pedal for you! "Maybe they'll give us a ride in a rickshaw."

My father took us over to the receptionist. "Good morning, Mr. Morgan, Mrs. Morgan, kids. I'm Margie," said a beautiful silken-haired Hawaiian behind the counter.

I leaned up against the wall and tried to sleep through the sound of another cheerful voice. If I'd been feeling better, I might have gotten annoyed at being called a kid by some-one who looked only a few years older than I am. But I was feeling so tired, I really didn't care.

"Right this way," Margie instructed. She led us through the door at the back of the plush reception area and into the bicycle garage. "Wait here just a second. I'll get Adam Gregory to show you around."

Margie jogged off to get Mr. Gregory.

Twenty carts with fringed canopies and leather seats lined the left wall. At least twice that many bikes stood in racks along the other wall.

"When do the riders come to work?" Stevie asked. "I want a ride."

"Uncle Mark said that the messenger ser-vice starts around ten, but the rickshaw cab-bies start taking passengers at eight," Mom replied.

"Ah, here comes Adam now." Dad pointed to the silhouetted figure walking toward us from the open back door. Margie was trotting along beside him. She had to take at least three steps for every one of his. He was at least a foot taller then she was.

"Mr. and Mrs. Morgan," Margie began as they reached us, "this is Adam Gregory."

"Pardon the grease," he said, shaking hands

with Dad. "I've been overhauling bikes since five this morning, and I still have three to go before we open."

"You're a very ambitious young man," Dad praised him.

Young is right, I thought. He was tall, but his voice sounded very young. "My brother Mark told me how good it was to have you in charge of all the repairs," Dad went on. "And I'm glad you'll be working full-time during your summer vacation."

Summer vacation? My ears perked up. He was in school? I peered past the grease smudges on his forehead where he had pushed his dark hair back. From what I could tell, he was pretty cute. Maybe there were possibilities here after all.

"Thank you, sir. I'm saving up for my college education. I'm happy to help out."

"To hear my brother tell it," Dad went on, "you're the only one around here who knows the front end of a rickshaw from the back. Mark says if it weren't for you, the riders would be picking up pieces of the bikes all along the Waikiki strip."

Adam blushed. "Well, I enjoy fixing things. And I'm real glad to have the job, sir."

How old is this guy? I wondered. He seemed younger by the minute. He'd barely looked at me when we were introduced. I stood up a little straighter and tucked my shirt into my jeans when his back was turned.

"Are you ready for your tour now, Mr. and Mrs. Morgan?" Adam asked.

"Lead on," Mom suggested.

Adam showed us the rickshaws and how they worked by giving Stevie a ride. "They're easy to pull for someone who weighs over a hundred and thirty pounds. That's why most of the rickshaw cabbies are college guys and most of the messengers are girls. Carrying messages to hotel guests out on the beach or delivering small packages doesn't take as much muscle."

"How late are we open?" Mom asked.

"If it's light, we're open," said Adam proudly.

"That doesn't leave much time for fun," I joked, hoping to get his bright green eyes turned in my direction. "I mean, if you work all the time it's light, when do you swim and surf and snorkel and stuff?"

He didn't say anything for a minute. Mom and Dad had walked on ahead, and Stevie was making vrooming noises next to a rickshaw.

"Work comes first," Adam said in a tone that made me wonder if he were eighty years old instead of a teenager.

Well, excuse me for even suggesting there

might be something fun to do around here, I thought to myself.

The cab driver had returned right on schedule. I caught up with Mom and Dad, and we all piled into the taxi again for the ride to Uncle Mark's condo. So much for Adam Gregory, I thought as we passed palm trees and beachfront hotels.

"Hurry up, gang. Let's get settled and hit the beach," Dad said excitedly when we pulled up in front of the building.

We lugged our bags to the third floor.

"I thought Uncle Mark owned a condominium. This is an apartment." Stephen stood blocking the doorway and surveying the tiny kitchen and small living room.

"Well, at least the plants are still alive," Mom commented before she answered my brother's question. "A condominium is any apartment you buy instead of rent, honey."

"How about moving out of the door, lardo?" I pushed him through. "These suitcases aren't light, you know."

"Where's my room?" Stevie asked as he headed back toward the hall.

Mom glanced at Dad. "There's good news and bad news, kids. The good news is that Uncle Mark and Aunt Mary said you could use their huge collection of computer video games while you are here."

"Oh, boy!" Stevie dropped his bags and ran to the television set.

I lowered my suitcases to the floor and waited for the bad news. It wasn't long in coming.

"There are only two bedrooms. You two will have to share."

"Mom!" my brother whined. "I don't want to sleep with her. She snores and—"

"Oh, pipe down!" I shouted. "Go complain in the closet. I'm going to take a shower and a nap." I stomped into the hallway and dropped my bags in the room with the bunk beds. The robot wallpaper made it pretty obvious which bedroom was ours.

Before anyone had a chance to argue, I locked myself in the bathroom and jumped into the cubicle-type shower. I let the hot water run over my head and neck and tried to relax my aching muscles.

I sighed. A long shower was just what I needed after a five-hour plane ride, a two-hour tour of the rickshaw business, a put-down from the first boy I'd met, and the wonderful news that I'd have to share my room with a nine-year-old. I wished I didn't have to wait a week to call Merry. I missed her already. I had visions of my exciting Hawaiian summer turning into my endless Hawaiian summer.

Three

"**H**OW can you be bored?" my father exploded. "We've only been here a week, Gina. I've barely unpacked, and you've already done all there is to do?"

"Yes, Dad," I explained patiently. "I've covered every inch of the beach. And I've been to the zoo, the muumuu factory, and the park concerts. If I have to sit through one more hula show, I'm going to grow a grass skrit."

Maybe this wasn't a good time to talk to my father. He had been interviewing new bike messengers all morning to fill two openings, and I don't think he'd found anyone.

"I need a job, Dad. I want something to help me keep busy and meet some kids." My gaze took in the seascapes lining the walls of the front office. Wherever you looked, on the wall or out the window, you had a view of the ocean.

"Isn't there something I can do around here? Dad, I love the ocean. But I need something to do besides sunbathe all day. I could organize the storage area so the rickshaws would be easier to get in and out in a hurry," I suggested.

He scratched his head and opened a button on his floral print shirt. "Adam does a fine job of keeping the place in order. What about baby-sitting other kids? Have you checked around the apartments?"

I didn't want to tell Dad that baby-sitting wasn't a good way to meet a guy. I glanced down at the string bracelet on my wrist. The color had faded a little, but I was no closer now to getting it taken off than when I'd left home seven days ago. I needed to be where the action was, and, I might add, without Stevie the pain.

I took a deep breath. "I hear you've been looking for messengers. Have you found anyone yet?" I asked cautiously.

"Nope. I've talked to girls all morning. None of them wants to work the hours I need—early morning through lunch. Nobody seems willing to get up at the crack of dawn."

"I love getting up before daybreak," I fibbed. "How about hiring me?"

He looked at me as if I were crazy.

"Hey, you said yourself that you weren't finding anyone. I'm reliable. I'm a good rider. I could do it. Please, Dad."

He shuffled the stack of applications on the desk. "What about watching your brother? You know you promised you'd take care of him on days when I need your mother in the office."

I had an answer ready before he finished. "If I only work until lunch, I could be back to the apartment before Stevie is even ready to go anywhere. You know he stays in bed until at least eleven reading comic books. By the time he's done getting dressed and eating, I'd be home. Come on, Dad," I begged. "Give me a chance."

"Okay, honey. I'll hire you on a trial basis for two weeks." He came around the desk and hugged me. We started walking toward the back room. "Run out back and ask Adam to show you the ropes. You can start tomorrow. How's that sound?"

Have Adam show me around? Yuck, I thought, remembering Adam's stuffy work-comes-first attitude. My gaze fell instead on two great-looking guys hitching their bikes to rickshaws. One was tall and blond. The other was shorter, but he was still taller than I am. He had black, curly hair. And they both had incredible golden-bronze tans.

"Adam's probably too busy." I waved my hand in the direction of the two boys. "I could just tag along with some of the rickshaw riders. They could tell me the streets and stuff."

Dad looked doubtful. "Go talk to Adam first. He knows more about this place than all the rest of us put together, including your uncle Mark, I think."

"I do want to start as soon as possible . . ." I took one more long look at the two cute guys and headed back to Adam's domain, the mechanic's shop.

I peeked around the corner. Adam, greasy and grimy as usual, was parked on the floor fixing a ten-speed. He was wearing cutoff jeans and a shirt that said Beach Bum on the back. He turned the bike upside down so he could spin the wheels. It was hard not to notice how his muscles bunched up and relaxed as he shifted the bike into the rack. He might be stuffy, but he is good-looking, I thought. Having Adam show me around might be nice at that, I told myself silently.

"Hi!" I entered the room and sat on a stool next to him. "Want to go for a ride around Waikiki?"

He shook his head, not bothering to look up. "I'm busy."

"Dad wants you to show me the streets and stuff. He's hired me as a messenger for a two-week trial."

"I really am busy right now."

My shoulders tightened. I folded my arms across my chest and tried once more. "I start tomorrow. I need a guide. Can't you stop working for a couple of hours and teach me what I need to know?"

"Use a map," he said. "You'll figure it out. Hey, you're sitting on my crescent wrench."

"No, I'm not," I replied, trying to keep my voice calm.

"Yes, you are." He looked at me finally.

"I do not have your wrench, Adam," I said. I jumped up and showed him the stool. "See!" I pointed. "I'm not trying to keep you from working. I'm trying to go to work myself. Dad hired me for mornings, and I intend to start tomorrow whether you show me what to do or not! I'll ask Ron or Jim out there. Maybe they'll have time."

"That's fine. Ask them. I really can't do it right now." He waved his arm at a stack of bike parts. "Three of the ten-speeds need new derailleurs. Two of the rickshaws need their bearings packed."

"The sun rises and sets, and you never go out of this garage. Why don't you just loosen

21

up and have some fun like other guys your age?"

I wasn't sure how old he was, but he couldn't have been as old as he looked. His height made him look older, just like me.

"Age has nothing to do with responsibility. Either you have it or you don't. And I'll bet that you don't even last your two-week trial period. You told me yourself that you hate getting up early. Well, be here tomorrow at six A.M. I'll give you a tour you won't forget."

"Fine! You've got yourself a bet."

"What do I get if I win?" His eyes gleamed like polished jade, almost as though he was having fun.

"If you win, I promise I won't pester you ever again," I offered. "But if I win," I said, bending down low to make sure he was paying attention, "you have to take some time off and take me someplace fun. Deal?"

We shook on it.

Now I had grease on my hands, too.

He stood up, filling the room almost to the ceiling. "Now where is that darn tool?" he asked himself.

I yanked open the door to the main garage. "By the way, Mr. Organization, your wrench is in your back pocket. You were the one sitting on it." I smiled. "See you at six."

I went back to the office to tell Dad that Adam couldn't take me until morning. He agreed to let me go with Ron and Jim, the two cute guys I'd been watching earlier.

I grabbed Dad's shirt and tugged him in the direction of the garage. "We'd better hurry if we're going to catch them before they leave on their shift," I urged.

"I'm glad Adam can fit you into his schedule tomorrow, honey. The other boys can help you with street directions and so on, but Adam's the one who knows all the procedures."

The last thing I wanted to be was a slot on Adam Gregory's precious schedule. So far, all I'd seen of him was a flash of grease as he flew from one task to another. He never stopped. I wasn't sure he even ate lunch. He might be cute, but he was so serious all the time. He was a work-o-maniac, and now we had this stupid bet. But don't worry, Adam Gregory. I'll be working two weeks from now despite your predictions. And I'll be having fun at the same time.

Ron and Jim were so different from Adam. They knew how to enjoy life. I'd seen them around the shop flirting with the messenger girls all the time. They talked about surfing after work and volleyball on the beach by moonlight. It would be easy to dream about one of them taking my bracelet off.

"Ron, Jim," my dad said. "This is my daughter, Gina. I've hired her as our newest messenger, and I'd like her to ride along with you two this afternoon to get a feel for the streets."

"Pleased to meet you." Ron grinned and tipped an imaginary hat.

"Likewise," Jim echoed.

They both looked me over. Chills of excitement ran up and down my spine. With my new shorts and matching print blouse, I thought I looked at least sixteen. There were advantages to being tall.

I straightened up and replied in my deepest voice. "Nice meeting you guys, too. Just let me grab a bike, and we'll be on our way."

I walked over to the bike racks, throwing a glance over my shoulder to see if they were still watching me. They were. I tossed my curls, then took my dark glasses out of my pocket and propped them on top of my head. This was going to be fun. I might have something to tell Merry during our phone call tonight after all.

Letting a mysterious smile play across my lips, I imagined our conversation as I walked the bike back to join my two companions. *Yes, Merry,* I would say to her. *Ron and Jim*

and I rode our bikes all over Waikiki. Then we
stopped for some snow cones, only they call
them shaved ice here. Then they invited me to
dinner and a moonlit volleyball party on the
beach. They couldn't decide who was going to
walk me home so they flipped a coin. Jim won.
It was under the palm tree in front of the swim-
ming pool that Jim brushed my hair away from
my face and . . .

"Have a good time, honey." Dad kissed me
on the cheek as we were getting ready to leave.

Ron saw the kiss, and I thought there was
definite interest in his warm gaze. Jim made
sure I had the route book very firmly in my
backpack before he finished zipping up the
message compartment. Yep. This was going to
be the best afternoon I'd had in a long time.

"Just remember, boys," Dad shouted as we
left. "Take good care of my girl. She's only
thirteen, you know."

Pow! My balloon popped. The rest of the
afternoon I might as well have been a deflated
piece of rubber for all Ron and Jim cared.
They might have been interested in me before
they knew my age, but now they were
embarrassed at having to be seen with me.
They said about two words to me and kept
staring at me like they couldn't believe how
young I was.

They had no trouble chatting with every female in a bathing suit that we passed along the way, however.

"Hi, honey," Jim called to a redhead standing at the bus stop. "Want a lift? Can you come to the game tonight?"

"Hey there, miss. Can you tell me where you bought your suntan lotion? Would you like to play on my volleyball team this evening?" Ron joked with a brunette coming out of a souvenir shop.

"I'd be happy to take you to the zoo and back," Jim told a blond who hailed us from the beach. "Sure, I'll go slow. I wouldn't want to mess up your beautiful hair. Say, how about joining us for a little supper and a game at the beach tonight?"

Finally the girl looked curiously over to where I was straddling my bike. "What do you need me for? Looks like you already have a date."

"No, Gina's not going to be there. You have to be at least fourteen to come."

It was terrible. It was humiliating. Even Adam Gregory and his schedule would be better than this.

Four

THE afternoon dragged on and on. I hardly noticed the silhouette of Diamond Head standing like a protecting shadow in the distance or the balmy breeze bending the coconut palms toward the sea. Sparkling sand crunched under my wheels as we passed view after breathtaking view.

I concentrated instead on acting cool and trying not to cry. I was determined not to show my hurt feelings to Ron and Jim. Finally, we parked our bikes back at the garage.

"Thanks for taking me, you guys," I called as they rushed out the door to their beach party.

"No problem, Gina. It was great having you!" Ron hollered just before the door slammed shut.

"Yeah, great," I choked out. There is nothing worse than being treated like a thirteen-year-old by two sixteen-year-olds. I sagged into the big, soft corduroy chair behind my dad's desk. Thank goodness tonight was the night I got to make my first phone call back home. I really needed to talk to Merry right now.

Merry answered on the second ring.

"Gina, is that you?" she asked. "Gosh, I'm glad you called. It's been murder not talking to you all week. How's Hawaii? Meet any cool guys yet? Still got your bracelet?"

"Hi, Merry," I interrupted her speech. She was so happy, I hated to burst her bubble with my sad story. I needed to talk to her, but it could wait a while.

Instead, I asked her what she had been up to. "Any of the boys in our class grow yet?" I joked.

"Well . . . as a matter of fact . . . do you remember Randy Brown?"

"He's the guy who transferred overseas with his family in fifth grade, right?"

"Yeah, well he got transferred back here, and he'll be going to our school next year."

"So what about him?" I asked. Merry always liked to string a story along for all it was worth.

She giggled. "He's six feet tall! Can you believe it? I saw him at the ice cream shop the

28

other day, and we ate our cones together. He's really cute now, not all bony with his hair sticking out like in elementary school."

I forgot my earlier bad mood and joined Merry in her excitement. After I got a thorough description of his statistics—color of hair, eyes, clothes, and bicycle—I asked the big question.

"Did he kiss you?" I held my breath waiting for her answer.

"Not exactly," she replied. "But he walked me home, and he would have if . . ." She trailed off.

I shifted around and leaned up against the fat arm of the desk chair. "Well, what exactly did happen?" I demanded.

"Like I told you. Randy walked me home. He even put his arm around me, just to help me up the steps. Well," she continued, and I knew she was enjoying the retelling almost as much as the event itself, "when we got up to our landing, he bent down like he was going to kiss me. But Mom opened the door at that very second."

"Gee, I'm sorry, Merry," I told her while secretly grinning. I couldn't help it. I didn't want Merry to be back in California having the time of her life while I was stuck in Hawaii being miserable.

"Anyway," she was saying, "Randy invited me to hike through Muir Woods this weekend, and you never know what might happen."

"Good luck," I wished halfheartedly.

"Anything exciting happening on your end?"

"No, nothing much. We're just barely settled in. I've been to a couple of hula shows, the zoo, and the muumuu factory. I'm working part-time for the shop."

"You're working already?" She sounded amazed. "Are you telling me you haven't met one interesting boy in a whole week? There must be thousands of boys stretched out all over the beach and working at the rickshaw service. You're just teasing me, right? You're trying to make me guess."

I thought back over the last few hours. I could tell her about Adam. No, she wouldn't want to hear about our fight. But, there were Ron and Jim . . .

I took a deep breath. "Now that you mention it, Merry, there was this *one* tiny incident. You see . . ."

I launched into a tale about the great afternoon I'd spent with Ron and Jim, two fabulously cute rickshaw cabbies who gave me the grand tour and then invited me to a volleyball barbecue at the beach this evening.

"Sorry," I concluded, "I'll have to fill you in

on the rest of the details after the party tonight. The guys are in front of the shop right now. I'd better go, Merry. Jim is motioning for me to join them for a swim before the party. I'll wait for your call next week. Say hi to Randy for me."

I didn't wait for her to ask any more questions. I just hung up. I slumped deeper into the chair.

How could I sink so low? I'd lied to my very best friend, because I couldn't stand it that she had found a boyfriend and I hadn't. I vowed to be honest with her next week and tell her that I'd made up the story about Ron and Jim.

I stood up and squared my shoulders in an attempt to shake off my gloom. So what if Merry was the first to find somebody special and have her bracelet taken off? I, Gina Louise Morgan, was mature enough to be happy for her.

My thoughts were suddenly and very rudely interrupted by a knock on the office door. "Come in," I called. A second later, Adam Gregory poked his head around the door.

"Hope I'm not disturbing you. I was looking for someone to help me hold the rickshaw I'm working on. You seem to be the only one here."

Adam stood in the last glow of the setting sun, waiting for me to volunteer my services. Copper beams bounced off his dark brown hair, turning it red.

"Do you lift weights?" I wished I could have taken it back the minute I'd asked, but it just sort of popped out. I'd never seen a guy with so many muscles.

"No, I lift bikes." His voice held a note of impatience, but his eyes crinkled for a second, so I could tell he was pleased that I'd noticed. "Are you going to help me or not? I'd like to get out of here. We have an early day tomorrow, in case you forgot."

"No. I didn't forget. How could I possibly forget what is sure to be the thrill of my young life . . . taking a tour of the city with you?" I said sarcastically. Gosh, Adam really brought out the worst in me. "In fact," I added, unable to help myself, "we'd better do this project quickly. I need my rest so I can keep up tomorrow."

"Look, I'd get your dad to help. But he's in the back talking to a tour guide about shuttling their hotel guests back and forth for a flat fee. An arrangement like that is always good for business, so I don't want to disturb him."

I tossed my head and flashed him what I hoped was a cold stare. "I'd be happy to help.

I work here, too, remember? Just lead the way."

"On second thought," he said, "I think I'll bring it out here. There's better light. Wait right there."

While he was gone, I wandered to the window. Across the street a bunch of high school kids were stringing the net for volleyball. I noticed Jim, with his arm around the blond we'd taken to the zoo, leaning over the barbeque pit. Where was Ron? I wondered.

Oh, there he was, setting up the lounge chairs.

"Here it is, Gina." Adam handed me two wheels. He held the axle and set a box of silver ball bearings on the linoleum floor behind the counter. "Hold this while I tighten the bolts," he instructed.

I kept track of the action out the window with one eye and watched Adam's sure-handed skill with the other. First he packed the hub with grease. Then he placed the tiny bearings around the ring.

I strained to watch the game across the street. The blond girl was a terrible server. I'm much better, I thought.

"Do you play volleyball, Adam?" I tried to make conversation.

"Uh huh."

"Think we could go join the game after we're done?"

"I have to go straight home. Hold the wheels still. You're pulling the axle out of alignment."

I went back to watching the game. Up and up the ball flew. One, two, three hits on Jim's team. One, two, and a slam on Ron's side. The blond was worthless. She covered her eyes when the ball came toward her.

Suddenly the ball streaked almost straight over the net, and Jim ran to intercept. He underhanded it with clasped hands, but I couldn't see if he made it or not.

I jumped up to see just as Adam raised the ring full of bearings. Crash! Steel balls rolled everywhere.

"Are you crazy?" he shouted. "Now I have to start all over."

"I'm sorry, Adam." I surveyed the mess. "Why don't we leave it, and I'll come in a little early tomorrow to clean up. It's pretty late anyway. You can finish fixing the rickshaw tomorrow."

"I had planned to finish the rickshaw today!" he sputtered between clenched teeth. "I have to train *you* tomorrow. Because of *you* I won't have time to do my regular work." He wiped the back of his hand across his forehead, adding another line of grease war paint.

"Are you sure you don't want me to help?" I dropped to my knees and started scooping up the bearings. The volleyball game didn't seem very important now. I bumped into Adam as we both reached for the same bearing. He jumped as if I had bitten him.

"Go home, Gina," he practically shouted. "I'll clean up."

I didn't know if he was more tired or angry, but I didn't stay around to find out. How could I ask? He just sat there like a statue until I left. My feet felt like lead on the way home. How could I have been so clumsy? Was there some way, I wondered, that I could make it up to Adam? Could we ever be friends?

Five

"I just can't get over the cost of food in Hawaii. I've tried every market in the area, and the prices are unbelievable," Mom announced as she came through the door carrying the groceries. Stevie was two steps behind, struggling with the second bag.

"You should have seen the chickens," she continued as I jumped up to help put the food away. "They were the scrawniest little things. I don't know what we're going to eat over here. Vegetables are sky-high. Even fruit," she said, laughing. "Papayas and mangoes are hanging all over the trees down Kapahulu Boulevard, but from the prices in the store, you'd think they were imported."

"Had a good time shopping, I see," I said with a smirk.

"You won't think it's so funny when we have to eat burritos five nights a week," she told me.

Stevie looked up from the computer screen to give his seal of approval. "That would be fine with me. I like burritos . . . and tacos, and enchiladas, and tamales, and tostadas . . ."

Mom threw up her hands in dismay. "Okay, Stevie. We know you like Mexican food."

Dad walked in at that moment. He'd stayed at the shop longer than I had since he was still working out the details of the hotel shuttle job.

"How was your ride with the boys this afternoon, honey? Have you got all your streets memorized and your landmarks pegged?" he asked.

I put on my best smile and tried to forget how awful my day had been. First there was my clash with Adam, then my humiliation with Ron and Jim. Merry's good news hadn't helped, either. And then to top it off there was the ball-bearing disaster with Adam. He probably thought I was the dumbest thing around.

"Fine, Dad. Everything went just fine." My stomach churned. Boy, if I didn't stop stretching the truth, my nose was going to start growing like Pinocchio's. I reached up and brushed the tip just to make sure it was the same as always.

"Did you enjoy your talk with Merry?" Mom asked. She handed me a head of lettuce and some other salad ingredients.

Well, what was one more lie on top of all the others? "Oh, sure, Mom. Merry's having a lot of fun with Randy Brown. You remember him from fifth grade, don't you? It seems his family moved back to Oakland, and he'll be going to our school next year again."

"That's nice. I'm glad Merry has found someone to pal around with while you're gone."

I couldn't bring myself to agree with that one, no matter how good my fib record was so far today. Instead I got really involved in ripping lettuce. It was a great way to get rid of frustration.

Dad munched on a piece of celery to the tune of Stevie's alien blips in the front room. "I was thinking today about a few ideas to make Ricki-Ticki Rickshaws a more profitable operation," Dad said. "I'd like to get your opinions on them."

"We're ready to eat. Why don't we all talk over dinner," Mom suggested. "Turn it off now Stephen, and come to the table."

"Aw, Mom. I've almost conquered the galaxy."

"Conquer it after dinner. It's time to eat."

Stevie blew up his last video ion cloud and stomped to the table. He soon forgot his aliens and proceeded to splash catsup on his hamburger, his french fries, and his string beans.

Oh, gross. I didn't even think I'd ever get over the fact that my brother ate catsup on everything. About the only thing he spared was milk. But that was only because he put grape juice in it and called it a purple cow. He wasn't satisfied with pure anything.

"What's your idea?" I asked Dad, trying to avoid watching Stevie dribble catsup out the sides of his mouth.

"What do you think of uniforms?"

"Uniforms?" we echoed.

"You know, so that our rickshaw cabbies would be recognizable from other companies doing the same thing."

"Uniforms would be more professional than cutoff jeans and T-shirts," Mom said.

"Exactly," he exclaimed. "I saw some nice gray slacks and white shirts with bow ties and captain-type hats in the mall. What do you think, Gina?"

I thought for a moment. "I think the idea of unifying the riders is good, but it's too hot for pants and ties. Besides no one would see gray across a crowded beach."

I looked down at my new outfit. "What about red? Red shorts, a yellow and red Hawaiian print shirt, and a red visor cap. We'd all look alike, and we'd be comfortable."

"Sounds good," Mom added. "I think you're right about the color scheme. You could write the words 'Ricki-Ticki' in bright yellow on the visors just to make sure."

"Another thing," I added. "What if we paint the rickshaws to match—red with yellow striped trim and a high flag with our name and slogan on it?"

We chewed and thought. Dad kept saying "Hmmm." Finally he put his fork down. "I like it. Yep. I like it. Mark said to do what I thought was best to perk up the business image, and I think Gina has made a great suggestion. We'll go shopping tomorrow to find just the right combination. How's that sound?"

We spent the rest of dinner talking over ideas for the shop. Dad also agreed that the garage needed to be reorganized for quicker dispatching of messengers. After dinner I wandered out on the lanai. That's the Hawaiian version of a balcony. I stretched out on the chaise lounge and let the balmy breeze lift my hair. I was glad something good had happened today. I wondered what Adam Gregory would look like in red shorts.

To the east I had a view of the hotel-studded skyline. Farther north the bald peak of Diamond Head darkened the night sky.

Below me was the parking lot of a small shopping center. Blinking lights drew my attention to the video arcade. Arcades were big in Hawaii. There was one on every corner.

"Hey, Stevie," I called. "Want to go down to the arcade for a few games?" There wasn't much else to do, so I might as well act like a big sister. I looked over at my parents to make sure it was all right. Stevie was already at the door.

"An hour, tops," Mom said. "You have to be up early tomorrow, remember?"

Actually, I had almost forgotten my morning date with Adam. If he thought he was going to wear me out riding around tomorrow, he was mistaken.

When we got to the noisy arcade, Stevie ran off immediately. I chose a game I'd never seen before and set it on the beginner's level.

I racked up a terrible score and entered my name on the list at the end of the game. The machine actually laughed. I had to smile at that. I glanced around to catch sight of Stevie and noticed he was talking to a tall guy holding a broom. I could only see the guy from the back, but he looked familiar.

Of course, I thought, it's Adam. I could tell by the back of his head. But what would he be doing here? He had a job all day. Don't tell me he worked nights, too? I marched my way through the crowd aiming directly for my brother and Adam.

"I can't believe you!" My amazement rang out in my voice. "Don't you get enough work at the shop? I've never met anyone so determined to make money . . ."

I had begun my lecture as I walked. Adam needed someone to slow him down, teach him that there was more to life than work. But the expression on Stevie's face had made me hesitate.

I couldn't figure out why he looked so strange, but that didn't stop me. I reached out and grabbed Adam by the sleeve and spun him around.

I froze. Now I knew why Stevie had looked so weird. The guy I was yelling at wasn't Adam. He wasn't even close. He was at least forty years old and had a potbelly and a beard. He was obviously the janitor for the video arcade, and I was a total jerkette.

Somehow the words wouldn't come for an apology, much less an explanation. I was embarrassed. I turned and ran out the door, yelling for Stevie to follow me.

Six

RED and gold fingers of sunlight were just crawling over the ocean horizon as Dad and I arrived at the shop the next morning. The Ricki-Ticki Rickshaw sign looked forlorn above the darkened office windows.

I had forgotten how early I would have to get up to be here before six. I shivered and stifled a yawn. Without the comforting warmth of the tropical sun, my carefully chosen shorts outfit made me feel like an ice cube. At least I had the satisfaction of knowing I had arrived before Adam.

Dad fumbled with the key while I took one more long look at the breathtaking beauty of the sunrise over the Pacific Ocean. Waikiki was especially gorgeous in the early hours before the crowds gathered.

Adam was missing a lot by working all the time, I thought. Maybe I could help him see that there was more to life than wrenches and ball bearings. But I still couldn't figure out why I wanted to bother.

"Good morning, Mr. Morgan, Gina," an overly cheerful Adam Gregory greeted us the moment we stepped from the office into the garage. "Glad to see you're on time, Gina. Ready to go?"

"How . . . how long have you been here?" I stammered. By my watch it was only five forty-five.

He grinned and pointed to a row of shiny rickshaws behind him. "Today is wash day. I came in a couple of hours ago to spruce them up before we took our ride. That way I don't lose so much time on the maintenance end by escorting you on a training mission."

I wanted to slap that smug expression right off his energetic face. Here I was barely dragging in on time, and he'd been here half the night.

"Your dedication never ceases to amaze me," commented my father. "I hope you're writing all this down on your time card."

"I hope you choke on your time card and your dedication," I mumbled sullenly.

"Did you say something, honey?"

"Nothing worth repeating, Dad," I replied sweetly. "Well, we'd better get going," I added for Adam's benefit. "I wouldn't want to put you too much behind schedule."

"Don't you worry about schedules," Dad insisted as we left. "I'll take care of dispatching messengers and whatever else comes up. You two enjoy yourselves while you're out, okay?"

In the time it took me to respond to Dad and wave, Adam was half a block ahead of me. No way was I going to ask him to slow down. He was determined to prove that I was worthless as a messenger, and I was equally determined to show him that I was capable of doing the job well.

This isn't going to be easy, I told myself, as I pedaled hard to catch up.

It didn't take us long to reach the hotel section. I followed Adam and tried to memorize the hotel and street names as well as directions. I knew I'd still need a map to do my job right.

"This is the Royal Hawaiian Hotel, the oldest hotel in Honolulu," Adam announced as we sped by about the twentieth location. "You pick up messages at the front desk. Find out where the person is supposed to be and what the person looks like. Then head for the beach or wherever."

The front of the Royal Hawaiian was

covered with native plants. The curved and drooping leaves blended perfectly with the curved pink structure of the hotel.

"Are those ti plants?" I asked, slowing to look more closely. I pointed to the small grove of short trees with umbrella-like leaves. "I read in the guide book that leaves from the ti plant were used for raincoats and food containers and fishing nets. Is that really true?"

"Yes, it's true," he answered reluctantly. "Ti stalks were also held up like white flags to surrender in battles," he called back over his shoulder.

"I just wondered," I said, pedaling to catch up again.

He rode on, making attempts at further conversation impossible.

"Here's the Coral Seas, the Edgewater, the Imperial Hawaii . . ." He continued to point to hotel after hotel along the main route through Waikiki. "Most of our jobs are within a five-mile radius. I've shown you the pickup spots, now let's head for the typical delivery stops."

"We've been riding for two straight hours, Adam," I yelled at his back as we passed several refreshment stands. "How about a little break before touring the beaches?"

He coasted until I came up even with him. "Tired already, huh?"

"No. But, I am a little hungry and thirsty. If I'd known we were training for the Olympics, I'd have brought a water bottle."

"I figured you wouldn't be prepared." He reached into his backpack and brought out a can of cola. Generic, of course.

"I suppose you brought a picnic lunch, too?" I snapped.

"No. I figured we'd be back before lunch."

"Well, I didn't eat breakfast," I told him matter of factly. "And I'm going to stop at the next hot dog stand and get something to eat. Go on without me if you want to," I offered.

I ordered my "breakfast." Adam stood tapping his foot on a low wall while he waited for me to finish eating. His gaze wasn't on me, though. He was watching the windsurfers hopping their rainbow sails over the breaking waves. Adam was really good-looking when he wasn't scowling. His nose was straight without any bumps, and his dark hair was neatly styled with just a hint of curl.

"Windsurfing looks like fun, don't you think?" I asked him. "Are you any good at it?"

"I've never tried," he replied. "Never had time."

I bit back a retort about his working so much. He must have some reason for the way he acted and why he worked so hard. I wondered what it was.

I finished my hot dog and touched his arm to let him know I was ready. "I'm fueled for the rest of our journey now."

"You'd better be. We have six more sites to visit." Was it my imagination, or was his voice just a teeny bit less edgy? He didn't jerk away from my touch this time. And was there the slightest hint of an answering smile on his lips? Maybe he just needed a friend.

We rode along in silence except when Adam pointed out locations. I gave up trying to remember everything and just enjoyed the ride. I loved the feel of the moist air rushing past my face and the challenge of trying to keep up with Adam. I was a good rider, so Adam never got very far ahead of me. We were fairly evenly matched.

We took Kalakaua Avenue around the base of Diamond Head. The street was called Kahala Avenue on the other side. My family had hiked up to the lookout tower above the crater last weekend and had battled the winds to get a look at the view.

"This is our last destination." Adam finally dropped back beside me and pointed down a steep cliff to a sandy beach bordering a crystal clear lagoon. "It's called Kahala Beach, and up there is Waialae Beach Park." He motioned farther up the coast. "Both tourists and locals come here and to Hanauma Bay to snorkel in the tide pools. This is as far as Ricki-Ticki will ride with a message."

I took a deep breath. I loved the smell of salt and suntan lotion. "Let's walk down to the beach, Adam," I suggested.

"It's a pretty steep climb. It isn't likely you'll ever have to come out this far, so I don't see any point in hiking down."

"Gosh, I'm surprised at you, Adam. This cliff looks like the perfect opportunity to prove that I'm not cut out for the strenuous demands of messenger work. Or maybe," I challenged, "you just don't feel up to the climb?"

He looked at his watch. "If we hurry, we can climb down and still get back to the shop before noon."

"What's the rush?" I asked, starting after him down the first gentle incline of the trail. "Dad said to take our time and enjoy ourselves. And don't give me that line about work being more important. You're working right now. You're training me, remember? You'd think you'd be broke if you didn't work or something."

"I would."

"You would what?"

"I would be broke if I didn't work. I don't

have parents who support me," he said.

That stopped me mid-step. I watched Adam make his way carefully down the rock-strewn path.

"Hey, wait up. Can I ask you a personal question?"

He kept climbing. "Go ahead," he said. "You will anyway."

"How old are you?"

He mumbled something that sounded like fourteen.

"What did you say?" I ran a couple of steps to catch up so I could hear him. That was a mistake. My foot hit a root that was stretched across the path, and I went flying.

Adam jumped the last four feet to the sand below. He turned around just in time to see me coming through the air. He reached up to catch me, but it was too late. We landed in a heap of arms, legs, sand, and backpacks.

"Are you all right?" He raised me up off his chest and started brushing the sand out of my hair. "What happened? One minute you were giving me the third degree, and the next you were tackling me. Are you sure you're all right?"

"I . . . I think so. Did you just say you were fourteen?"

"That's right. Let me help you up." He

offered his hand. "Any bones broken?" he asked, a note of true concern in his voice.

Suddenly he was being very nice. He ran his hands along both of my arms. Then he twisted my neck this way and that. "You appear to be okay," he said.

My gaze met Adam's, and he slowly dropped his hands from my neck to my shoulders and then down to his sides. I felt warm all over. Maybe I was okay on the outside, but I wasn't sure about the way I felt inside.

Seven

MY arms still tingled where Adam had felt to see if my bones were still intact. He's just fourteen, only one year older than I am. Hawaii was looking better all the time. I had a hundred questions to ask, but I kept my mouth shut on our ride back to the rickshaw shop.

I couldn't get what Adam had told me on the trail out of my head. Why didn't his parents pay his way? Didn't he have parents? Didn't they work? Maybe they couldn't work.

"Hey, Adam," I started to say, but he cut me off.

"If you're worried that I'm going to tell your father about your accident back there, don't," he said.

"Actually, I was going to ask you another personal question," I ventured.

"Not while we're riding, please." He

gestured to the traffic. "You seem to get into trouble when you try to talk and do anything else at the same time."

I swallowed my reply. What good would it do to apologize for the ball bearings or the tumble down the cliff? He already had an opinion of me, and it wasn't a very good one. How was I going to get him to change his mind?

There was something about Adam Gregory that I really liked, despite his attitude. I was more than a little curious about his background. There had to be a reason that he acted so tense all the time.

By the time we arrived back at the shop, it was past lunchtime and I was starving again. Adam didn't say a word. He just headed straight for his workshop the minute we walked in. I started to follow, but Dad stopped me.

"How was your ride, hon? Are you ready for your first assignment?"

I took one last look at the swinging door to the garage and turned back to Dad.

"I'm as ready as I'll ever be."

"Good." He handed me a canvas envelope full of messages. "There's a party on Waikiki beach in front of the Royal Hawaiian Hotel. Do you know it?"

I nodded.

"A group of conventioneers are out there. They'll all be wearing red hats. Take these messages to the coordinator. His name is Jack Michaelson. He'll distribute them."

"Will do." I saluted and rode off. I still hadn't had lunch. In fact, I thought I was only supposed to work until noon. Oh, well, Dad was the boss.

I spotted the red-hatted group right away and pedaled right up to the head luau table. "Would you tell me where to find Mr. Jack Michaelson?" I asked the woman on the end.

"He's down there taking a hula lesson." She pointed to four people wiggling their hips and flailing their arms around, trying to imitate the motions of the hula teacher.

"Jack Michaelson?" I inquired of the four. Two people turned around, an older man, and a boy about my age—tall, thin, and good-looking. "I have some messages for you." I held out the package.

"Take care of it, son." The older man slapped the younger one on the back. "I think I've almost got the hang of this."

"Are you both Jack Michaelson?" I asked. "Because the rules say I have to deliver this personally to the recipient whose name appears on the message."

"It's okay," said the younger one. "We're

both Jack, although you can call me J.T." He stuck out his hand to shake mine, and I dropped the package. We both reached down to get it and bumped heads.

"Now I can call you black and blue. Sorry about that," I said apologetically.

He grinned. "Listen, anything's better than having to do that dancing stuff. In fact, you're the best thing that's happened to this party since it started. Want to stay and have lunch with me?"

I looked around at the group. J.T. was the only young person there. "I really should get back . . ."

"No, you shouldn't." He smiled again and steered me in the direction of the buffet table. "You look hungry. And I'll bet you haven't had roast pig all day. Please?" he begged. "Save me from total boredom?"

"Well, why not?" I smiled back.

We loaded up our plates and sat on a sand dune overlooking the party. "Where are the rest of the kids?" I asked between bites of tender pork and sweet roll.

"I'm the kids," he informed me. "My folks insisted that I come with them. They said I would enjoy Hawaii, but so far all I've seen are planned luaus and tours. I hadn't met anybody my age until you came along. What's there to do here, anyway?" he asked.

I laughed. "You're talking to the wrong person. I'm a tourist, too." I explained how we were in Honolulu running my uncle's business while he spent the summer in Europe. "I got bored taking care of my little brother and touring muumuu factories, so I went to work as a messenger."

"Too bad we're not going to be here longer. I'd get a job, too."

"How long are you going to be here?" Maybe there are some possibilities here, I thought.

"One more week with my parents' friends, and then we're staying for another week on our own." He scooped up a glob of poi, this gray pasty stuff, on his spoon, and devoured it. "Want to come swimming with me tomorrow? We could even try windsurfing if you like."

He glanced up to catch my answer. "Are you making that horrible face because you don't want to go out with me or because I'm eating poi?" he asked. "I'd hate to think it was because of me."

"No, you're right. It's the poi. I know Hawaiians love it, but how can you stand to eat that stuff? Not only does it look disgusting, but it tastes like sandpaper."

He took another bite. "It's not so bad once

you get used to it. I figure when in Rome—I mean Hawaii—do as the Hawaiians do. And you didn't answer my question." He waited.

"Oh! Sure, I'll go swimming with you, and windsurfing, too. I've been dying to try it. I have to work until noon, and I have to ask my folks, but it should be okay." One thing was sure. If I waited for Adam to take me anywhere, I might be waiting forever.

We exchanged phone numbers and I headed back to the shop feeling happier than I had since we arrived. Now, finally, I had something interesting to tell Merry when she called Friday.

* * * * *

I was right. The week really did go fast with working in the mornings, baby-sitting in the afternoons and spending time with J.T. Sometimes I had to take Stevie along with us, but J.T. didn't seem to care.

We went swimming in the hotel pool. Then we did some windsurfing, which was fun, even though it took me about a hundred tries to get going. But once I got the hang of it, I didn't have any more trouble. I even won a race with J.T.

Suddenly it was Friday, and the phone on

Dad's desk was ringing.

"Hello?"

"Hi, Gina. Merry, here. Are you in a better mood this week?"

"Much better," I assured her. "I've been seeing this guy named J.T. Michaelson. Well, his real name is Jack. But that's also his father's name, so they call him J.T."

"Slow down, slow down. Has he kissed you yet?" Merry got right to the point.

"Not yet. We've just been having fun." I didn't mention that he'd gone home today.

"What about Ron and Jim and the volleyball match? That sounded like a real romance brewing there. I've got so much to tell you, too, Gina."

I was just about to tell Merry that the story with Ron and Jim was all a lie, but something stopped me. Something in the tone of her voice when she said she had "so much to tell" me.

"My news can wait. Tell me about Randy," I said.

She giggled. "Randy's so great! We went roller-skating in the park. Then he took me to Wonder World and we rode all the rides. Well, you know the ride called the Pirate's Tunnel?"

"Go on," I encouraged.

"Randy kissed me when we were in the

tunnel. I thought I'd die," she went on. "My heart was beating so hard, I heard the echo in the tunnel."

"Gee, that's neat, Merry." I tried to sound enthusiastic. "Did he take off your bracelet?"

"Of course he did," she gushed. "How about you? Ron or Jim kissed you, right? Oh, isn't it great that it happened for both of us the same week? I guess that means it's a tie. No more contest, huh?"

Merry would be so disappointed if I told her the truth, I reasoned. What harm could a "little" exaggeration cause? She'd never find out.

"Actually, Ron and Jim practically had a fight over who was going to walk me home that night," I invented. "Jim won. They had to toss a coin."

"Oh, Gina. That's so neat!"

"Right. Yeah, well . . . so Ron—I mean, Jim—walked me home and stopped me under the coconut tree in front of the apartments. And, well you know the rest."

"Did you have trouble breathing, too? Did your knees go weak?"

"I'm weak all right."

Merry detailed her trip to Wonder World with Randy, and I wished I was strong enough to tell her that nothing had happened that night. Instead of Ron and Jim and J.T., I should have told her about Adam. But I only saw him when I received my messages in the morning and when I returned my bike to the garage. There wasn't much use in wanting someone to like you when that person barely knew you existed.

"Are you listening, Gina?" I heard Merry ask. "I've asked you the same question three times."

I came back to earth. "Sorry, Merry. I was thinking about something."

"Or someone," she tacked on. "I asked you what time you'll call next week. Same time?"

"Same time. Say hi to Randy for me."

"I will. I'm so jealous. You've got paradise and three guys," she said. "I guess I'll have to settle for just one."

"Three's not so wonderful," I told her. "I'd rather have just one good one."

Eight

"MOM, can I ask you a question?" I slid my lounge chair over next to her at the condo pool. Stevie was doing tricks off the diving board, and I had just climbed out to dry off after doing twenty laps.

Mom put down her book. "Sure, honey. What's up?"

I plunged right in. Mom and I had always talked about everything, even guys. "What could I do to get Adam to like me more?"

"Why do you think he doesn't like you? He seems like such a nice boy. He's always helpful. Always doing a good job for the business."

"That's the problem," I admitted. "He does too good of a job. He works all the time. I don't think he ever relaxes. Do you know he sometimes comes in at four o'clock in the morning? He's only fourteen years old."

"That does seem a little early for someone

so young," she agreed.

"He's there really late at night, too. And weekends," I added. "He told me his parents don't support him. He has to earn his own college tuition money. He's always telling me I'm in his way, that he has to work."

"Well, maybe he just needs a friend."

"I was just wondering if his parents are poor or something. Maybe we could help them out? Give his dad a job or something," I suggested.

Mom thought for a moment, a frown creasing her forehead. "Oh, no. I don't remember exactly what David told me, but I'm sure the Gregorys aren't broke. In fact, I think Adam's father is an executive. Maybe Adam works so hard to show his father how responsible he is. Maybe he doesn't get along with his father the way you do with yours. I'm just guessing, of course. Why don't you ask Adam?"

Somehow I couldn't imagine walking up to Adam and asking how he got along with his father.

But I was more curious than ever to find out what Adam was really like.

* * * * *

I had time to think about it for two whole days. On Sunday, our family drove around

66

Oahu to visit the Japanese gardens in the Valley of the Temples.

The Byodo-In Temple was a great place to think. All Stevie wanted to do was ring the giant *bunsho* bell that hung at the entrance. I wandered off to sit among the carefully arranged plants and study the beautiful fish swimming in the reflecting pools.

It was so quiet there. My body felt as if it were floating along with the swans down the shimmery brook and under the carved wooden bridge. I heard another tourist say that there were ten thousand fish in the pool that I was watching. If only Adam could sit here for a while—take off his shoes and feel the quiet. Maybe he would stop being so serious all the time and relax a little.

"A penny for your thoughts." Dad sat down on the stone bench next to me and tossed a fallen leaf into the water. We watched it slowly edge its way to the pond.

"I really like Hawaii, Dad," I found myself saying. "I like the weather and how the trade winds are always blowing so you stay cool even when it's hot. I like swimming in the ocean and working at the shop . . ."

"But?"

"But," I said, smiling over at him, "I miss Merry and my other friends. Talking on the phone just isn't the same."

"You and Merry didn't have a fight, did you?"

"No. It's just that she seems to be having so much fun without me. She's met Randy, and now they're going to movies and Wonder World and stuff. I can't stand to tell her that nothing like that is happening to me."

"So what did you tell her?"

Dad had a way of getting to the point.

"I kind of made up a couple of stories about some of the guys at the shop. I know I was lying, but I couldn't stop myself. Now she thinks I have three boyfriends. She's all excited that we both found boys at the same time. I just can't tell her the truth."

Dad's strong hand covered mine. "What do you think you should do? I know you'll do what you think is best."

My parents always let me try to figure things out for myself. But this time I just wanted them to take care of it so I wouldn't have to.

As we left the Valley of the Temples, I decided to begin telling the truth starting Monday.

Nine

"**O**KAY, quiet down, everyone," Dad shouted above the noise in the shop. "Let's see what you all look like in your new uniforms."

The cabbies and messengers all turned toward Dad. "You look great," he exclaimed.

There were murmurs of approval from around the room where thirty high school and college kids stood in their red shorts and yellow tropical print shirts. Each one wore a red visor cap with the words "Ricki-Ticki rides for U" written in bright yellow across the brim.

Adam stood in the back of the room with just the shirt of the uniform tucked into his regular old jeans. I wandered back to where he stood with his hat and shorts in hand.

"How do you like the new uniforms?" I whispered while Dad was giving his pep talk about how the new image was going to bring us tons of new business and instant recognition.

"I hear they were your idea."

"Uh huh. Dad thinks it will really unify the riders and create a much more professional appearance," I said, a note of pride creeping into my voice.

"Well, I'm not wearing it," he stated flatly.

"Dad says everyone has to."

"Not me. Why should I? No one sees me in the garage, and I'd just wreck these adorable little shorts working in grease all day." He held the red material in front of my nose between pinched fingers.

He had a point. "You're right," I conceded. "I'm sure my father will make an exception in your case."

His mouth dropped open. "Did I hear you correctly? You actually agreed with me?"

"Is that so hard to believe?" I asked.

"I just expected an argument, that's all. We usually don't agree on many things."

That was what I wanted to change. "Maybe we got off on the wrong foot. How about if I make it up to you by helping you paint the rickshaws tonight? Dad wants to see the whole image as soon as possible, and you'll be here all night if you have to do it alone."

"Thanks. I appreciate the offer," he said quietly.

And I appreciated the chance to show Adam that I could be useful and responsible, just like him.

* * * * *

"Do you think we can get all twenty done this evening?" I stood, paintbrush in hand, surveying the garage full of empty, unhitched carts. Each cart had two big wheels and a long metal bar sticking out in front that hooked underneath the seats on the ten-speeds. Luckily, Dad said we didn't have to paint the bikes, yet.

"It depends on how late the others plan to stay," remarked Adam, who was holding a paint can as well as a brush. "Let's start on this one. We'll tip it up on end. I'll take the inside, and you take the outside. Okay?"

"That sounds like a good plan to me."

Four other riders and my parents and brother had stayed to help us paint. Mom was keeping Stevie busy refilling paint buckets and stirring the newly opened cans of candy apple red paint.

Adam and I worked well together when we weren't fighting. We had done two carts before the other teams had finished their first ones. So far we had worked in silence except for the slosh and dip of paintbrushes.

As we started the third rickshaw, Adam began humming. "What song is that?" I asked after trying to guess through three choruses. The sound of Adam's voice was nice.

"It's a song my mother taught me when I was little. She used to sing it while she worked. It's called 'When Irish Eyes Are Smiling.'"

"Is your mother Irish?"

He went on painting for a moment before answering. "My mother was Irish. She died when I was eight."

"Gosh, I'm sorry. I can't imagine how hard it must be to grow up without a mother."

"I'm used to it now," he said. "It was harder on my younger brother and sister and on my father. Dad hasn't been the same since."

I wanted to ask why, but I didn't want Adam to think I was prying. He was really nice when he wasn't yelling at me.

To keep the conversation going, I took a different approach. "I didn't know you had any brothers and sisters. You never mentioned them before." I laughed. "I'm always complaining about Stevie. Did you know that I have to share a room with him while we're here? It's awful. Yesterday I found a half-eaten peanut butter and catsup sandwich in his sock drawer," I said, laughing.

Adam laughed with me. "I'm lucky to have my own room. We all do. In fact our house is so big I rarely see my family, even when I'm home. We're not close like your family."

There it was again. An invitation to find out more about the real Adam Gregory, but I still held back. A little voice inside my ear told me to wait a little longer.

"I do know what you mean about little brothers, though," he continued as we moved on to our fourth cart. "Michael drives me nuts with his train set all over the garage floor. Half the time I can't even get my bike in and out to come to work. But I always know where he's been, because he leaves a trail wherever he goes."

"He sounds like Stevie, only Stevie's trail is usually food."

Our paintbrushes stroked in unison. Up and down, up and down. Dip and start again.

"What does your dad do?" I finally asked.

"He's the president of a bank. Honolulu Savings."

Okay, I thought, here goes. "If your dad is a bank president, why do you have to work so hard? And why did you say you wouldn't have any money and wouldn't be able to go to college if you didn't work?" This was Adam's chance to tell me to mind my own business. I crossed my fingers and hoped he wouldn't.

As usual, he painted a while before answering. I was getting used to the deliberate way that Adam Gregory did things. He thought everything out before he spoke or did something. When we had taken our tour last week, he had our route and itinerary planned out right down to the minute.

"My father is a self-made man. His family was poor, but he worked hard and put himself through school. He wanted a better life for his family. He expects me to do the same. I don't get an allowance, and I have to earn my own spending money and save my own money for college. And he's right," he added. "People who get everything handed to them don't appreciate it as much as someone who earns every penny."

"But what about the good life your father wanted? It sounds as if you both work all the time and never see each other or do anything as a family. What good is the future if you don't enjoy at least some of the present?"

He sat back on his heels and wiped his paintbrush against the inside of the can. He seemed to be deep in thought. His eyes were focused on something other than the rows of finished rickshaws.

When he finally spoke, his voice cracked a little. "My mother was in charge of keeping my father from working too hard. She was the one who always insisted that he come home for dinner and take weekends and evenings off. We did lots of fun things like beachcombing and having coconut-shelling contests." Adam smiled, remembering. "It's different now, but I know my father loves us. That's why he works so hard."

"Is that why you work so hard, too? Because you love him?" It was just like my mom had said at the pool. He earned more than money. He earned his dad's respect and love.

"You may be right, Gina Morgan." Before I could stop him, he punctuated his statement with a blob of paint on the end of my nose.

A second later, I aimed my brush for his nose in reply. Unfortunately, he turned his head and I ended up painting a red stripe across his cheek.

He jumped up, overturning the last few drops of paint in the can. "Why, you!" he shouted, smiling broadly. He pulled back the bristles on his brush and spattered my old T-shirt.

"Who said you could decorate my shirt?" I held it out for his inspection. The whole thing had already been smeared with paint, but I blamed him anyway. "Look at this mess, and it's all your fault! Take that! And that! And a little of that!" I shouted back as I painted zigzags on his arm.

"You've had it now!" was the last thing I heard him say. Suddenly, we were chasing each other around the garage, waving our brushes over our heads, and splashing paint all over each other.

Pretty soon everyone was in on the act. Mom painted Dad on the ear. Stevie got Mom on the hand. Ron and Margie were after Jim and Diane. It was a free-for-all, and the paint was winning.

"Let's call it quits," Dad yelled during a small break in the action. He looked silly lecturing us with red blotches all over his face and paint apron, but we settled down. "Before we destroy all our fine labor," he said, pointing to the twenty shining rickshaws, "let's clean this mess up and head for the beach. We can cool off and wash up at the same time. Then I'll treat you all to shaved ice. Deal?"

"Deal!" someone shouted. We all got busy cleaning up. Thank goodness most of the mess was on bodies and plastic drop cloths.

Adam and I grabbed the paint can at the same time. A tiny bit of paint got on my wrist, the one with my string bracelet on it. Adam carefully took a corner of his shirt and wiped the spot off, holding my hand as he did it.

Our eyes met again like they had at the beach. Very large butterflies did acrobatics in my stomach. This time I was sure he felt something more than plain concern. After all, why should he be so worried about one little drop on my wrist when my whole arm was already bright red?

"Why do you have this string tied around your wrist?" He lifted my hand. "You've had it on since you came. Are you trying to remember something?"

What was I supposed to say? I was surprised enough that Adam had noticed anything about me or what I was wearing. I could have made up a story. Instead I opted for the truth.

"Actually," I began, "it's sort of dumb. My best friend and I each have one. It's only supposed to be taken off by . . . someone special." I looked up hopefully.

"Oh," he said finally, and changed the subject quickly. "Well, we'd better finish cleaning up. If we're going to wash this paint off in the ocean, it will be easier if it's not too dry."

"Right." I sighed and followed him to the trash bin to toss the rags and cans. So much for the truth.

Ten

THERE was only one more week until Merry and her family were due to arrive in Honolulu. What was I going to say to her when she showed up and I had no real boyfriend to substitute for the imaginary ones I had been telling stories about all summer? The minute she laid eyes on Ron and Jim she was going to know nothing had ever happened between us.

And then there was Adam. Things were really starting to go well between us until I told him about my bracelet. I should have taken it off right then and there to show that it didn't mean anything to me.

Adam had barely talked to me since that night. He'd talked to all the others during our swim and afterward at the shaved ice stand, but he'd ignored me.

My two-week trial period at the shop had ended, but Adam hadn't even teased me. He'd probably been too busy to notice I'd stuck it out and won the bet. Today, though, he couldn't ignore me. We were all going to Waimea Falls Park.

I hummed while I helped fix a picnic lunch. "It was really nice of Dad to ask Adam to go with us," I mentioned to Mom. "Do you think I should make him one sandwich or two?"

"Two, dear. He's a growing boy. Better make two for all of us. Your father says we'll be doing a lot of hiking, and you know how hungry this family gets."

Mom put pickles, olives, carrot sticks, and celery sticks into separate plastic containers and stacked them in the ice chest. "Good thing I baked this batch of cookies yesterday. You never know when your dad is going to get one of his ideas. This time I think he's feeling guilty that all we've done is work since we've been here."

"Yeah. With only a couple of weeks left he wants to make sure we've seen a tourist attraction or two."

"You never know," Mom said mysteriously. "We may have more time than you think to do our sight-seeing."

Just as I turned around to ask her what she meant, Dad walked in with Adam and Stevie. They were all laughing it up over some joke

Stevie was telling—something totally unfunny, I was sure.

The ever-present Hawaiian breeze rippled through the windows over the sink, blowing the paper cups off the table. Adam and I both reached to grab them. Our heads bumped, knocking us back on our heels. I lost my balance and ended up on the floor. I must be naturally clumsy around guys. I'm always running into someone.

"Are you okay?" he asked, rubbing his head.

"I'm fine." I was also rubbing the spot where our heads had collided. Adam grinned and helped me up.

"What are you guys smiling about?" Stevie interrupted our moment. "Don't your heads hurt? I heard your bones crunch all the way over here."

Adam handed me the paper cups. "We're just smiling at your joke, Stevie," he said quickly.

"Yeah, Stevie." I looked at Adam and smiled. "Tell it again. I didn't hear the whole thing."

For the first time in my life I listened to one of my brothers stupid jokes and cracked up. I knew it was going to be a great day.

We arrived at the nature area and spent the morning as a group watching demonstrations of poi making and basket weaving. We all went swimming in a beautiful pool filled by a waterfall. Some of the island children were climbing up the cliffs and diving off.

After lunch, Dad checked the park schedule and suggested we go our separate ways until the dancing show at four that afternoon.

"Let's meet at the front entrance," Dad instructed. And I could have kissed Mom when she grabbed Stevie's arm and made him go with them.

"What should we do first?" I asked when Adam and I were finally alone. We were standing near the front entrance by a pond filled with lily pads.

"Oh, I don't know." He studied the brochure. "If we want to go on the tour, we have to wait here for the next tram. If we want to go to the exhibits . . ."

I stared at him. He was doing it again, planning every detail. "Adam," I said. "Don't take this personally, but you're just too organized. I can see I'm going to have to take charge of this expedition.

"See that Indian village up ahead?" I pointed to a group of thatched huts and piles of stone ruins.

"Yes. You want to go to the Indian ruins? Fine with me."

"I don't just want to go," I said. "I want to race! I'll bet I can beat you to the village."

He hesitated.

I took off.

I had gone at least thirty feet when I heard him behind me. His running shoes barely made any noise on the leaf-strewn path, but I knew he was sprinting to catch up.

No way was I going to let him beat me. I ducked under a branch and pounded up the stone steps to the village. Adam was only a couple of strides behind.

"I won!" I shouted between breaths.

He was barely winded. "You had a head start."

"I can't help it if you stood there all day thinking about it."

"You're crazy. Do you know that?"

"Crazy's not so bad." I smiled.

"Speaking of winning," he added seriously. "I have to admit I didn't think you'd make it as a messenger. I was wrong. You stuck it out and won the bet."

I didn't know what to say. I didn't expect Adam to ever admit defeat. But there was something different about him today.

"Well," I told him, hands on my hips, "I still expect to collect. And today doesn't count."

"I don't mind losing," he said, his eyes

locking with mine in a silent message.

"Hey, what are all these round nuts on the ground?" I asked, to keep my mind off his windblown hair and flushed cheeks.

"Kukui nuts. The natives used them for money, oil, and jewelry. That's what those shiny black necklaces in the tourist shops are made of."

I picked up one of the grayish brown nuts. "Well, the finished product sure looks a lot different."

"The nuts have to be polished for days." He picked up a nut, tossed it in the air, and peered into a hut.

Meanwhile, I collected a handful of the nuts and ducked down behind a rock. "I know something else they're good for."

"What's that?" He looked around.

I aimed a kukui nut at his feet. Pop! It hit the toe of his shoes.

"Hey!" He quickly grabbed a handful and ran behind a tree. A second later he was bouncing nuts off the rock I was hiding behind. He was throwing the little things so fast I couldn't get a toss in.

"No fair!" I shouted.

"You started it," he called back.

He must have gone looking for more nuts, because suddenly I had a chance to throw a few myself. Plink! Plink! Plunk! I tossed fifteen or so.

"Give up?" I yelled. "I've got you now!"

"Nope," said a voice very close behind me. "I've got you."

He pinned my arms to my sides. "Drop your weapons," he growled.

My kukui nuts clattered to the ground. I could feel his breath on my neck. And hot and cold chills were running up and down my arms where he touched me.

"I can see that I'm going to have to hold on to you to see that you behave, Gina Morgan."

I struggled . . . sort of.

Inch by inch his hands moved down my arms. He picked up my wrist with the bracelet on it. Slowly he ran his finger under the string. I was sure he would feel my pulse hammering under his light touch.

"Do you need this anymore?"

"No-o-o," I said shakily. "It . . . it's only supposed to be removed by . . ."

"I bet I could snap it off with one finger."

"Uh huh," I managed to choke out. I wanted to turn around and gaze into his eyes. I stared at his fingers wrapped around the string on my wrist.

Pop! Adam broke the string. He turned me around to face him. His lips were so close.

Only a breath away.

It was just one kiss and only for a second. It felt like the sun blinking through the trees above us. Like the freshness in the waterfall pool. Like a thousand breaking waves against the shore. And I didn't once think about Merry or our bet.

Eleven

ALL week long, all I thought about was Adam. I kept hoping there would be a chance to tell him the whole dumb story about the bracelet, but the moment was never right.

Unfortunately, I hadn't had a chance to tell Merry the truth, either. We'd had to cut our call short because my family went out on Friday night. Oh, well, I'd have plenty of time to tell her about Adam when she arrived on Monday.

"You're sure deep in thought." Adam sneaked up behind me and placed his hands over my eyes. "Guess who?"

"Godzilla?"

"Nope."

"King Kong?"

"Wrong again."

"I give up," I said, and giggled.

"Well, I'll tell you then. It's your friendly

neighborhood bike mechanic who is looking for someone to go riding with him this afternoon."

"I have to take care of Stevie." I couldn't believe it. Adam was actually taking time off for fun.

"That's okay. Bring him along," Adam offered. "And wear your swimsuits. But come over here first. I want to introduce you to someone."

Adam led me out of the office door and into the dimness of the garage. Two boys were standing by the rickshaws. The older one had been talking to my dad.

"Gina, this is Brett and his brother Paul," Adam said. "They just moved into the house next door to ours. Brett was looking for a way to earn a little money before school started, so I brought him down here."

We said hi to each other. Brett was our age and Paul was nine or ten like Stevie.

Dad broke in. "I've just hired Brett to fill Rick's spot, since Rick is leaving to go back to college. You came along at just the right time, Brett. Welcome aboard. I know Adam and Gina can show you the ropes this afternoon."

"Excuse me a minute, you guys. I'll go call my brother. We can ride by and pick him up on our way. And I can get my camera, too." I smiled at Adam and the other two, who were already chatting about routes, sights to see, and sports.

So today was going to be work, after all, I thought. But that was okay. I'd never seen Adam so friendly. I realized that he had changed since our trip to Waimea Falls park. He came out of his workshop more often, and he occasionally took time to ask how everyone was when he gave out morning assignments.

Every day was getting better and better. In fact, I wasn't really looking forward to moving back home.

I let Stevie know that we'd stop by for him. A short time later, the five of us were all out pedaling along the main strip past the same hotels and beaches that Adam had shown me two months before.

"Look over there, Brett." I waved toward the Doggie Diner. "They have the best hot dogs in all of Waikiki. Don't even bother buying from a stand on the beach. It's worth the extra time to eat lunch here."

"And over there," I continued, "is the best beach. Hardly any tourists go there, so the sand is clean, and the windsurfing is great!"

Brett laughed. "I thought Adam said your family only moved here this summer. You sound like you've lived here all your life."

I thought about what Brett said as I wove in and out among the pedestrians. We finally turned on Kapiolani Boulevard to get out of the crowd of people. I actually felt as if I *had* lived in Hawaii all my life. California seemed far away, and I liked the warm, sun-kissed Hawaiian ocean better than the freezing shores of San Francisco Bay.

"Your father said to take the rest of the afternoon off, so why don't we ride up to Hanauma Bay and go snorkeling?" Adam asked. He told the younger boys how far it was and asked if they thought they could make it.

"Sure!" they shouted in unison.

So off we rode, around Black Point and past Kahala Beach, the farthest point Ricki-Ticki delivers. We rode on around the island until we reached the most beautiful tide pools I'd ever seen.

Stevie and Paul ran off to catch crabs. Adam and Brett and I rented the snorkeling equipment. We joined the other snorkelers in the clear shallow waters that reached practically as far as the eye could see out into the protected bay.

I took a picture of Adam holding up a sea cucumber and squirting Stevie with the water inside. Then I snapped a shot of Brett and

Adam carrying Paul out to deeper water and dumping him in headfirst. Suddenly it was very important to have pictures of my friends, of the places we had been, of the fun we were having. Too soon, we would go home, and all this would be over.

"Hey, Gina! Stop playing photographer and dive in." Adam came striding toward me, his wet hands reaching for my camera.

"Let me put the camera in my bag. I'll be back in a minute."

I was really glad to see that Adam had found a friend in Brett. When I leave, he'll have someone to talk to and to keep him from working so hard, I thought.

Quit thinking about leaving, I told myself as I walked back toward the water.

Stevie was whispering something to Paul and Brett.

"Now!" he yelled. In a flash the two nine-year-olds were on me. Each took a hand and started pulling me toward the deeper water.

I fought back. "Forget it, you two. I'll get in under my own steam."

"Need some help?" Adam called.

"Adam, don't you dare!" I warned, while pulling hard against the tugs of the younger guys. "I'll get in myself."

Adam kept coming toward me. Brett was

right behind him. "Time for a swim," Adam announced. He took a flying leap and tackled me around the knees. My feet flew out from under me and I landed, plop, on the sandy bottom.

Of course I had to get back at him, at all of them. I stopped feeling sorry for myself and slammed the heel of my hand into the water, aiming for Adam's face.

He ducked and the fountain of water hit Brett. Brett retaliated, but missed me and got Paul. Pretty soon we were all having a great time. Boy, I was going to miss Hawaii.

Twelve

"WHAT am I going to do when you go back to California?" Adam lamented as we parked our bikes back at the garage.

"Maybe we can stay," Stevie said hopefully. "I'll ask Mom and Dad."

I looked from Stevie to Adam, wishing the impossible.

Adam reached over and squeezed my hand. "I wish you could stay, too."

At the airport a few days later, I was still wishing. We were waiting for Merry's plane. I held Adam's hand and thought about last week, the most wonderful week of my life.

How fast the time had gone. In between snorkeling and bike rides, Adam told me all about his school. He took me to meet his family. His father seemed nice enough, but the more he talked about Adam's accomplishments, the more I understood why Adam always worked so hard to please him.

Adam's father had even commented on the change in his son since Adam had met me and started having a little fun. Adam almost fell over when his dad announced that he was going to start taking weekends off to enjoy life a little more.

"Son," he had said. "We've both been pushing ourselves too hard. It's too bad this little lady isn't staying around longer to keep our noses off of the grindstone."

I agreed. I thought it was too bad, too. But Adam would have Brett to do things with. For a while, I'd been jealous of Brett's growing friendship with Adam, but I wasn't anymore. Brett was so much fun. It was hard not to like him. He was working today, or I would have brought him along to meet Merry's plane, too.

Memories of morning beach strolls and our afternoon of snorkeling at Hanauma Bay warmed me. I swayed in time to the Hawaiian music being piped over the airport loudspeakers.

"I can't wait to meet your friend, Merry." Adam nudged me as her plane rolled up to the walkway.

"I'm sure you'll like her." I wished I'd had a chance to tell Merry about Adam. Boy, was she going to be surprised. I was sure we would have a good laugh when I told her about all my fibs over the phone this summer.

"Here they come. First ones off the plane." Dad waved at Mr. Jackson. "I hope he brought the legal papers."

"What legal papers?" I asked Mom, but she was running off to greet Mrs. Jackson and to give her the lei she had brought.

"Gina!"

"Merry!"

We hugged and then checked each other out to make sure we hadn't grown.

"Merry, I have so much to tell you. You . . ."

She wasn't listening. She was eyeing Adam. "Aren't you going to introduce us?"

She walked past me right up to Adam. "Wait a minute. Let me guess. You must be Ron."

Adam shook his head, puzzled.

"Jim?" she continued. "J.T.?"

I swept past her and took Adam's arm. "Merry, this is Adam Gregory." I gave her a piercing look, hoping she'd act natural. "He works at the shop with me."

"Hi, Adam," she gushed. "Gina never told me about you," she blurted out.

Adam looked at me and back at Merry.

I pulled Merry by the arm. "Come on. You're luggage will be arriving." I had to get her away from Adam and explain the situation before she said something I would regret.

I thought I'd get a chance to talk to her on the way to the baggage claim area, but Adam kept the conversation going. "Did you have a good flight?"

"Yeah. In fact, I won the contest for guessing how long the airplane was, but they wouldn't give me the bottle of champagne for a prize because I was underage. They gave me an island cookbook instead."

"Just don't make poi." I made a face. "It's really overrated."

"We're in luck," Mrs. Jackson said to her husband as we rounded the corner to the baggage area. The luggage from our flight is already on the carrousel."

"There's my bag," Merry pointed. "The big blue one."

She reached out to grab it just as Adam leaned over to help. "Here, let me," he offered. As she withdrew her hand, I noticed something strange. Merry was still wearing her string bracelet. But she had told me that Randy took it off.

As fate would have it, Adam noticed her bracelet, too. "Oh, you're wearing a string bracelet, too," he commented as he set her suitcase down. He smiled a secret smile at me.

"Oh, this old thing?" She flipped her wrist this way and that. "Yeah, Gina and I made a bet at the beginning of the summer to see which one of us could get a guy to take it off first. Wasn't that silly?"

"Merry!" I gasped and looked at Adam, but it was too late. The damage had been done.

A moment ago Adam had been smiling. Now his eyes flashed sparks of anger. "That's all I was to you? A way to win a bet?" he gritted between clenched teeth.

I reached out to lay a hand on his arm, but he pulled away. "Adam, I can explain. It isn't like that, really."

"Maybe you should explain it to Ron," he said. "Or Jim. Or J.T. Or whoever else you tried to capture first. I'm going back to work."

I watched him walk away, then I turned back to Merry, who was looking a little confused.

"What did I say?" she asked.

"Too much," I told her. "Way too much."

It wasn't until that night after dinner that Merry and I had a chance to sit down and talk.

She followed me into my bedroom. "Okay, what's going on? You've been moping around since this morning like you lost your best friend. I thought *I* was your best friend. I'm still here, Gina. Want to talk about it?"

"Oh, Merry," I sobbed, tears spilling down

my cheeks. "I really like him. Now he hates me. He thinks it was all just a game."

She put her arm around me. "I'm sorry. How was I supposed to know you were that close? You haven't said a word about Adam during our telephone calls."

"I made up all of those stories to impress you," I cried. "I never kissed Ron or went to the volleyball match with Jim. And J.T. and I were just friends. Most of the time I spent with him, Stevie was with us.

"It's just that you and Randy were having so much fun," I continued, "that I didn't want you to know how miserable I was. So I lied. I'm the one who's sorry. If I'd told you about Adam, none of this would have happened."

Suddenly I realized that Merry was crying, too. "I lied, too," she admitted through her tears. "Randy never kissed me. I saw him at the ice cream shop that first day, and we went to Wonder World together and to the movies. But he didn't kiss me. It wasn't the romantic fantasy I told you about."

"What about Muir Woods? Did you make that up, too?"

She nodded her head. "Mom would never let me go to Muir Woods alone with a boy. In fact, she and Dad sat two rows behind us when we went to the movie."

I had to laugh at that. "There's no way he could have kissed you with them watching."

She giggled, too. "Well, once he did reach around the back of the seat and accidentally touch my shoulder with his popcorn cup."

"What a thrill," I teased.

"Hardly. I promise I won't ever lie to you again," Merry sniffed. "That bet was the stupidest thing we ever did."

"You're right. Let's make a better pact this time. Let's always tell the truth to each other, even if it hurts."

We hugged to seal the deal. It took us another two hours to tell each other what really happened over our summer vacations.

"What am I going to do now, though?" I moaned. Talking to Merry still hadn't solved my problem. "How am I ever going to get Adam back?"

Thirteen

THANK goodness I didn't have to work the week that Merry's family was visiting. Seeing Adam every day would have been too much to bear. The few times that I had caught a glimpse of him from the front office, he had turned and walked away.

We saw Brett, though. He and Merry hit it off right away. He hung out with us a couple of evenings and went to the zoo with us one day. The only thing we couldn't talk him into was the muumuu factory.

Today we were lounging on the private beach in front of the Jackson's hotel. A couple of kids were chasing waves, but other than that we were the only people there. Brett wasn't with us, and as much as I liked him, I was glad. He and Merry always had such a wonderful time together that I couldn't stand to watch. It was too depressing.

"You have to talk to Adam," Merry insisted. "You have to tell him how you feel."

"You saw the way he looked at me this morning when we stopped by the office. It's just not fair. The first time I find someone I really like, I lose him because of a stupid bet," I moaned. "He probably thinks I'm a total jerk."

She rubbed sunblock on her dark skin. "And he'll be right if you don't go talk to him. You have to tell him that he means more to you than any dumb bet, and that none of the other boys meant anything to you."

"Easy for you to say. Brett took off your bracelet after he knew the whole story. I'm the one who has to face Adam."

"Here." She handed me the bottle. "Stop worrying and do something useful. I can't reach the middle of my back, and I don't want to get burned."

"It always amazes me that black skin can burn." I rubbed her back and looked thoughtfully at my own arms, which had turned a toasty shade of copper during my months of messenger riding.

"This is the best tan I've ever had," I said to Merry. "I wish there was someone here to show it off to." I sadly looked up and down the beach, knowing I wouldn't see Adam's familiar cutoff jeans, but hoping just the same. I sighed heavily.

"Not to change the subject, but do you know what the joint family meeting is all about tonight?" she asked.

I stretched out beside her. "Nope. Our parents have had their heads together all week, but they haven't let any clues slip. I heard something about floral deliveries and legal papers. You don't think they're selling the shop back home do you?" I suddenly wondered.

"I doubt it," Merry said. "I heard my dad tell your dad that the florist business was booming. It must be something else."

"I guess we'll find out tonight."

I forgot all about the family meeting as I dozed on the beach. All I could think about was Adam. Somehow I had to make it right with him before I left. Even if we were never to see each other again, I wanted us to at least part friends.

* * * * *

"Will the joint family meeting come to order," Mr. Jackson said in his best judge-like voice. "David, you take the floor first."

My father stood up. "I know you're wondering

what all the hush-hush negotiations have been about this week." He addressed us kids. "Well, we have an announcement to make. Ricki-Ticki Rickshaws will soon be adding a new type of delivery to its routes."

"Ice cream?" Stevie asked hopefully.

"Sorry, son. But you're close. What makes people feel loved anytime, day or night?"

This was beginning to sound like the floral shop's motto back home. "Flowers?" I spoke up. It was hard not to feel better when Dad turned on the charm.

"You've just answered the million-dollar question. Flowers!" Dad exclaimed. "Ricki-Ticki will soon be adding floral deliveries to its messenger service. Flowers will bring in more of the local customers as well as appeal to the tourists."

"Your uncle Mark loves the idea," Mom added. "Especially since *we* will be moving here to Honolulu to run that part of the operation."

We're staying! my brain screamed. "You mean I'll be going to school here?" I tried to keep the joy bubbles from bursting out of my mouth.

"You'll start next week," she said. "I've already sent for your records."

"Where will we live?" Stevie asked my next

question. Oh, please, I begged silently. Let me be going to Adam's school.

"As a matter of fact we'll be living right in this building," Dad told us. "There's a three-bedroom unit for sale. If everyone agrees, I'll put down a deposit."

Later, after the family had discussed every tiny detail of the move, Merry and I lay across my bed working out a few plans of our own.

"I guess we're not going to see each other for a few months again," I said sadly.

"You won't miss me as soon as you get back together with Adam. Now you'll have a real good chance."

"I will too miss you," I assured her. "But at least we'll have the phone calls."

She nodded. "Yeah, maybe you can let Brett talk for a few minutes every time you call."

"No problem," I told her. I knew she was feeling the same way I was, only for different reasons. She had said good-bye to Brett earlier in the day.

"But the best part is the last plan they talked about at the meeting," she continued. "That we would maybe lease the California shop and move here so we could open other Ricki-Ticki delivery services on the other islands."

I lowered my chin onto my hands. "Do you

think that will ever happen? It seems like a lot of work," I commented.

"You know our parents. When they want something, they go for it," she said. "I hope so, anyway. I don't like having an ocean between us. And tomorrow I have to go back."

"Let's stay up all night. I'm sure your folks will let you stay overnight here," I suggested, "since we're taking you to the airport in the morning."

Somewhere around three A.M. we fell asleep, but morning came too fast, anyway. "I'm going to miss you even more this time," I whispered to Merry as I hugged her good-bye at the gate. "I'll call next Friday at our regular time."

Through tears, Merry whispered back, "Remember our promise. We're going to always tell the truth, no matter what. I want to hear what happens with Adam . . . even if it's bad."

Even if it's bad, I repeated to myself on the way back to the shop. The truth probably would be bad, I thought, after I fulfilled my second promise to Merry. I'd told her I'd talk to Adam . . . today!

Well, there was no time like the present. Adam was just walking back to his workshop as I entered the garage. I followed him.

I stood for a moment in the doorway. He

was too busy organizing tools on his pegboard to notice me standing there. Gosh, I'd missed him. He probably hadn't missed me, though.

"Darn!" he shouted. "Where did I put that wrench?" He rummaged through the drawers. "Here it is. What a stupid place to put it. Where's your head, Gregory?"

"I hope it's on your shoulders," I said softly. "I sort of like it there."

He spun around, wrench in hand. For a second, I almost thought he was going to throw it at me. He slowly lowered the wrench to the counter, then waited.

I took a step into the room. "Are you still mad at me?" My fingers clenched and unclenched in my pockets. Beads of sweat ran down my back.

He took a step toward me. "No," he said. "I missed you too much to be mad. Every time I tried to get you out of my mind, I ended up thinking about you every minute."

"You missed me?"

"Yeah. I told myself I'd be better off without you, because you're only going to leave anyway. But it didn't do any good. I'll be lost when you go back to California. I won't have anyone to yell at around here."

A smile tugged at the corners of my mouth. "Is that all you missed? Having someone to yell at?"

He, too, stood with his hands in his pockets. "A couple of other things, maybe."

"Those other guys didn't mean anything to me, Adam. I just made up stories to impress Merry. After we talked, I found out that she'd made up a few stories of her own."

Adam was quiet for a second. "So, you didn't kiss me just to win your bet?"

Warmth spread up my neck, remembering. "Believe me, the bet was the farthest thing from my mind."

"What was the closest?" He took another step toward me, closing the distance between us.

"Whether you were going to know that it was the first time I'd been kissed," I told him truthfully. The truth was beginning to feel pretty good.

His eyes were wide with surprise. "Me, too." He laughed and then grew serious. "I've never had a girlfriend before. I guess I've been just like Dad since Mom died. I spend all my time working instead of being with people. I wasn't really mad at you all those times this summer," he explained. "I was more mad at myself. I knew you were right about my working too hard, but I didn't want to admit it."

"I just wanted to be your friend, Adam."

"I know." He shuffled his feet. "I was just afraid of liking you too much and then having you leave me." He looked away.

"Like your mother did?" I interrupted softly.

He perked up. "I guess so. I never thought about it like that, but you're probably right. You're pretty smart, aren't you?"

"If I was really smart, I would have figured you out at the beginning of the summer. Then we wouldn't have wasted so much time," I joked, trying to lighten the mood.

He pulled my hands out of my pockets and held them. "If I kissed you again, what would you be thinking?"

I grinned. "Try it and see."

His lips touched mine, and the last week of pain and worry washed away. I didn't notice the grease on his forehead or the smell of the workroom.

"Well?" he inquired.

"I was thinking what a great year it's going to be."

His brows knitted together in a silent question. "We're moving here," I told him happily. "My parents are buying an apartment in my uncle's building, and Ricki-Ticki is going to start delivering flowers as well as messages."

He stood like he hadn't heard me. "You're staying?" he finally asked. "You're really staying?"

I smiled and nodded. "You can bet on it!"

About the Author

CINDY SAVAGE lives in a big rambling house on a tiny farm in northern California with her husband, Greg, and her four children, Linda, Laura, Brian, and Kevin.

She published her first poem in a local newspaper when she was six years old, and soon after got hooked on reading and writing. After college she taught bilingual Spanish/English preschool, then took a break to have her own children. Now she stays home with her kids and writes magazine articles and books for children and young adults.

In her spare time, she plays with her family, reads, does needlework, bakes bread, and tends the garden.

Traveling has always been one of her favorite hobbies. As a child she crossed the United States many times with her parents, visiting Canada and Mexico along the way. Now she takes shorter trips to the ocean and the mountains to get recharged. She gets her inspiration to write from the places she visits and the people she meets along the way.